For Grandman – G.A.

For Philippa – S.H.

Text copyright 2003 by Giles Andreae
Illustrations copyright 2003 by Sue Hellard

Published by Bloomsbury, New York and London
Distributed to the trade by Holtzbrinck Publishers

Library of Congress Cataloging-in-Publication Data:
Andreae, Giles, 1966-
My grandson is a genius! / by Giles Andreae; illustrated by Sue Hellard.— 1st U.S. ed. p.cm.
Summary: A grandfather describes the many precocious talents of his two-year-old grandson,
noting the child's possible similarity with himself.
ISBN 1-58234-815-4 (alk. paper)
[1. Grandfathers—Fiction. 2. Pride and vanity—Fiction. 3. Stories in rhyme]
I. Hellard, Susan, ill. II. Title.
PZ8.3.A54865 My 2003
[E]—dc21
2002026227

First U.S. Edition 2003

1 3 5 7 9 10 8 6 4 2

Bloomsbury USA Children's Books
175 Fifth Avenue,
New York, New York 10010

My Grandson is a
Genius!

by Giles Andreae

illustrated by Sue Hellard

BLOOMSBURY
CHILDREN'S
BOOKS

My grandson is a genius!
It's plain for all to see,
I'm sure it won't be long
Before he gets a Ph.D.

I know he's only two years old
But when you watch him play,
It's obvious he'll be
A famous scientist one day.

And although it sounds unlikely,
If you heard my grandson speak,
You'd probably elect him
As the president next week.

He's clearly very musical,

'Cause when he takes a snooze
He wriggles to the rhythm
of Gershwin's "Monday Blues."

And when you see him walking

It's embarrassingly clear

That he'll be in the Olympics
Not much later than next year.

He moves so very gracefully
For such a tender age,

And his voice is so angelic

That he'll really suit the stage.

His paintings are so masterful
You couldn't fail to tell
That my grandson and Picasso
Would have got on very well.

And when he kicks a ball

You'd be hard put to deny

That any player ever

Has had such an expert eye.

Though I'm not much one for boasting,

If you saw his little face,

You'd agree that they should use him

To promote the human race.

Yes, my grandson is a genius
And, though I'm not sure I'd agree,
His parents sometimes say
That he's a little bit like me!